GIVE ME AN
-A-

CHRIS M. HAWTHORNE

iUniverse, Inc.
Bloomington

GIVE ME AN A

iUniverse books may be ordered through booksellers or by contacting:

iUniverse
1663 Liberty Drive
Bloomington, IN 47403
www.iuniverse.com
1-800-Authors (1-800-288-4677)

ISBN: 978-1-4502-8669-5 (pbk)
ISBN: 978-1-4502-8670-1 (ebk)

Printed in the United States of America

iUniverse rev. date: 2/3/11

Preface

Give Me an A

This is a story that will break the hearts of millions -- boy meets girl, falls in love, and lives happily ever after -- NOT.

This story is full of betrayal, lies, revenge, and death. How far will a person go to get what they want?

By the end of this story, you make the choice-- was it for sex, greed, prestige, or was it just because it's like that and that's the way it is?! The most powerful thing God gives to mankind is the power to choose what you do! The choice is never good or bad, it is the choice that has the power over what you do not -- the act, or betrayal, or even love. Some people will do whatever it takes to get what they want. Trust, honesty, and kindness, are reversed for lies, cheats, and deception. Now the choice is yours -- enjoy or reject the challenge to choose the right thing.

Give Me An A

CHAPTER I

THE INTRODUCTION

Growing up in a small, country town, everybody knows everybody, and I thought that I could have the life that everyone dreamed of. This is my story! My name is Cody Taylor. All through school, I was the center of attraction. I felt I could have anyone and anything I wanted until I laid my eyes on Ebony. She was everything I always wanted—meek, quiet, pure, not like all the others, or so I thought. We became high school sweethearts. We did everything together—laughed, cried, made love, but were never apart for a long period of time. My senior year, I broke my leg, and that blew my scholarship at the University of Southern California (U.S.C.). I graduated and had one dead-end job after another. I managed to land a job at a microchip company and the boss liked me and made me a manager. As for Ebony, she got a job working in a bank as a loan officer.

One day, a long, white Mercedes pulled up to the bank and stopped. A tall, black man in a long, black leather coat got out and went inside. The minute his and Ebony's eyes met, it was like magic or a fatal attraction. He told her that he was a producer for one of the largest magazines in the world, and he thought she had the look that they were looking for to place in the upcoming issue in the magazine.

"Excuse me for staring," he asked, "but, what is your name?" As he sat down in her office, they began to chat. He asked, "How would you like to make mad money?!"

Ebony replied, "Excuse me, *Misterrr. . .*"

"Terry Donovan, but my friends call me T.D. It's a thing from back in my football days, you dig?"

"Yeah, yeah, I know, and next you are going to tell me that you would have gone all the way pro if you would not have broken your leg, hurt your back, and strained your knee."

"Whoa, whoa, you got me all wrong. I got tired of being banged around on the field. Oh, I had all the scouts to come out and see me play, and I had them all begging, and I just walked away. Growing up in Mississippi in my day and time, your chances and choices were limited to farm work on a hog farm or factory work in a blazing hot factory with a red neck telling you I don't pay you to talk, I pay you to work BOY!"

"Ha, ha, ha. So, what turned you into a big time magazine producer, or did you hit the lottery and build your empire from the ground up like the Jefferson's? Ha! Ha! Ha!"

"Oh, we are full of jokes aren't we? I got the same opportunity that I am trying to offer you, but if you are not going to take me seriously, I guess I'll just make my transaction and move on."

"Yeah, maybe that's what we need to do, SIR! How can I help you?"

"I need you to wire five hundred thousand dollars to Miami to a producer for the video T.V. show we are going to make on our upcoming star for the magazine."

"Five hundred thousand dollars? WOW! And, how do you plan to pay for this, Mister Big Time Money Man?"

"I have this—an unlimited gold card. I think that will take care of it Miss All That!"

"Why didn't you have your secretary to do this?"

"Well if you must know, I gave her a vacation in the Greek Islands for her hard, dedicated work and as a token of my appreciation."

"Here's your confirmation, Ebony, for the transaction."

"Thank you, Joyce."

"Well, I am impressed, Mr. T.D."

"Oh, look at the time, I must be going. Here take my card, and if you find it is not a joke, give me a call, and we'll talk. Bye, bye."

"Girl who was that?!" exclaimed one of the girls in the office. "Did you see the amount he wrote that wire for? He was quite amazing to say the least. Is he married, single, or what Ebony?"

"All I know is he is quite interesting to say the least."

"Ooooo, you go girl. Where's the digits?!"

"Girl, please," said Ebony.

Ring. Ring. Ring.

"Hey, boo, ready for lunch? Your choice!" said Cody.

"Oh, hey, baby, yes, I am ready to get out of here, it has been a wild morning."

"Check it out, my boss said if I keep up the good work at the factory, I might be moving up to twenty dollars by next month. Ebony, Ebony?! Are you still there?"

"Huh? Yeah, yeah."

"Wow, counting all that money all day must have really worked on you today. You sound like you are in the twilight zone."

"It's nothing. I'll be waiting."

"Lunch, Ebony?" asked Joyce.

"No, I am waiting on Cody. Ah, I see him pulling up now. Chow."

"Hi, boo, how is it going?"

"It has been wild in that bank today."

"They best not be working my baby hard because I will come and smack that bank president around, ha, ha. What's up baby? You haven't said a word."

"Oh, it's nothing," replied Ebony.

"I am going to be working over tonight, so I won't be able to come see you tonight, baby, but I will make it up to you, I promise, okay?"

"No problem, Cody. I am burned out and could use the rest, a glass of wine, and a good book—that will put me right to sleep."

Ring. Ring. Ring.

"Cody!"

"Yes, sir, Mr. Powell."

"I need you back right away to the site."

"Yes, sir, Mr. Powell—on the way! Well, baby, duty calls."

"What about lunch?"

"I promise I will make it up to you when I get this big check for this job. Sorry."

Kiss. Kiss

"I love you, and don't let that old bank stress my baby out, okay? Bye, bye—love you."

"Yeah, yeah, right, get out of here you! Ha, ha, ha. I love you too, boo."

"I will call you later!"

Zooooom.

"Cody, this is one of our new workers that has just started with us. I need you to show her how to operate the label press maker and bring her up to speed."

"No problem, sir. I will take care of it, sir, right away."

"Hi!"

"Hi! My name is Cody. What is yours?"

" Sam."

"Why is a gorgeous lady like yourself named Sam?"

"It's short for Samantha."

"Oh, now that makes sense. Out of all the choices you could have been a model, actress, singer, you name it, why did or how did you end up here?!"

"Yeah, like promoters were just beating down my door right. It's a long story."

"Okay, I feel you, let's get to work."

"Cool. "How long have you been here, Cody?"

"Too long, but, it pays the bills. Mr. Powell not so bad—just do your job and you'll be fine."

Sam ponders and says to herself, wow! This Cody is fine. I have got to get to know more about him.

****

"Morning, everyone."

"Morning, Ebony."

As Ebony logs onto her computer, it says, you've got mail.

"Hi, it's T.D., how is the banking business going? I just wanted to thank you for helping me get the money transferred for that account. It saved me a lot of headaches and paperwork. Oh, my offer still stands, if you decide you would like to make the money instead of counting other people's money. Let me know, and I will see what I can do for you, chow."

Ebony replies, "Look, Mr. T.D or whatever you call yourself, Mr. High and Mighty Man, I will survive in this poor little bank, sir, but, we thank yah sir, ha, ha, ha. Bye."

T.D. types back, "Just think about it, you'll be glad you did, yah hear?"

"Well Mr. T.D., we all can't be as lucky as you self, now can we? You're welcome. I was just doing my job. You do know what that is don't you? A job, T.D., or should I call you Mr. T.D.? Ha! Ha! Ha! Just kidding I will think about your offer, chow."

"Wait! If you decide call me on my private line, it's on the bottom of the card. Peace!"

"Ebony was that Cody? It was *Him* wasn't it?" Ashley asks.

"Yes."

"Girl, what are you going to do?"

"Please don't say anything to Cody."

"Girl, you don't have to worry about me—it is our secret."

"There is no secret; it's just business, okay?"

"Whatever, but you need to take advantage of this chance of a life time, it may not come again! At least think about it, Ebony. This could be your big chance, girl."

"Let's just get to work, and we can talk later about big chances and being a star and all that kind of jazz. Ha, ha, ha. Girl, you so crazy!" said Ebony.

"One last question," said Ashley.

"What, what?"

"When you blow up, can I be your manager?"

"Oh sure, sure, and you can also go with me on Oprah and David Letterman, and oh, oh, Jay Leno. Ha, ha, ha. Real funny, real funny, ha-ha."

"Well I know I would not hesitate if it was me. Well hold up a minute, where is it?"

"Here it is."

"What?"

"The number to Mr. T. or Mr.T.V. or whatever his name was, and let him make you a big star. It's that easy."

"Really?!"

"Hell no! Listen, all these type of guys all do the same thing. They drag you out to some big city and promise you the stars, bright lights, movie stars, dah, dah, dah, and when the dust settles, you are strung out, wore out, or thrown out."

"You're just scared of leaving your boo, Cody."

"Even if I didn't have Cody, the answer would still be the same hell no!"

"That's it, I am through trying to help you, " said Ashley.

"Thank you for not helping me help me, okay? Now can we get to work?"

"Yes, boss."

CHAPTER 2

"Hey! Hey! Hey, Cody, wait up! I never got the chance to thank you for showing me how to work the label maker. I am all thumbs," said Sam.

Beeep.

"Hello! Hi, honey, I am not going to be able to make our lunch date. We are having a long meeting at the bank in the boss' office. I hope you are not mad at me. Kiss, kiss," said Ebony.

"No, I'll just get a peanut butter sandwich and call it a day. Ha, ha, ha. Just kidding, I'll see you tonight," said Cody.

"Yes. Thanks, bye, boo!"

"Okay, bye, honey, " replied Cody.

"Sounds like someone got stood up for lunch," said Sam.

"No, she had other plans."

"Good, I owe you. Let me buy you lunch for helping me the other day at work."

"No I was just doing what I'm paid to do."

"Please, my treat! I won't take no for an answer."

"Okay, you win, I'll go! I'll go," said Cody.

"Oh, oh," said Sam.

"What now?!" asked Cody.

Sam replied, "I don't know where to go. Ha, ha, ha."

"I'll drive. Do you like barbeque?"

"I love barbeque!"

"Well, let's go! I know were the best barbeque in the world is."

"O yeah?! Show me, Mr. Man."

"No problem, Ms. Lady. Here we are—Lulu's Barbeque ''N Ribs. This is the best barbeque in all Saint Louis. Two specials, please. Here you go."

"Mmmmm, this is delicious."

"I told you."

"Well the food is good, but what do you do around here for fun?"

"Well, in the day time, not much goes on around here, but at night, we like to go to the mall."

"The mall? But, what do you do in the mall that is fun?"

"Not the mall. Inside of the mall there is a club called Shakers, and all the stars of hip hop and R&B go there to perform."

"So, do you go to this club, Shakers?"

"Sometimes."

Cody's phone rings.

" Hello?"

" Hi, Cody. The boss man said that the drive belt on the compressor stopped or broke or something, I don't know."

"Okay, Alvin, I'm on my way back. I'll be there in a few minutes. Well, duty calls."

"Yeah! I know. You the man, Cody."

"Sometimes I wonder if that is good or bad, you know?"

****

"Glad you are back."

"What happened?" asked Cody.

Alvin replied, "It just slowed down."

"Look! The hydraulic fluid line has a leak in it. We will have to shut it down to replace it."

"Did you say shutdown?!"

"Yes, sir, Mr. Finkell, we can't remove the hose until the pressure is released from the line."

"How long are we talking about?" said Mr. Finkle.

"Hour or two."

"WHAT?!"

"Yes, sir. We first need to see if we have it in stock and then drain the hose, and then build the pressure back up to get the line back up."

"SHIT! That could take all day! "We can't afford that! Send everyone home. That's a wrap."

Beep, beep, beep.

"Hello?!"

"Cody, I've got to work over at the bank because the audit team is coming Friday."

"Ebony, it must be a virus because I will be here on my job for at least two or three hours, or longer trying to fix this power line. Sorry."

"I know. See you when I get home."

"Okay. Bye, bye."

"Love you."

Ring. Ring. "Damn!"

"Hello, Ebony?"

"Yes."

"This is Donovan. I am glad I caught you. Remember I stated I had big connections? Well, I've got you a photo shoot with Black Star Magazine, the number one magazine cover for all the stars."

"Wow, wow, I never said I would do any shoot for a magazine."

"Well, I guess you couldn't use ten thousand dollars for about one hour's work."

"Say what?"

"You heard me, honey."

"Did you say ten thousand dollars?!"

"That's right, but if you don't want it. . ."

"I, I, I, never said I didn't want it. But, how? When? Where?!"

"You leave all that up to me; I will take care of everything."

"Wait!"

"Yes?"

"What about my job?"

"It's only an hour. I will fly you down and you will be back at work the next day."

"For real?!"

"Ha, Ha! Yes, for real. I must say, hey, with T.D., stars are made every day. Boom!"

****

"Ouch! Did you get it, Cody?"

"No, this nut is stripped. I'll have to cut it off."

"NO! The pressure is building back up. What the?!"

"Sorry, Cody, but Mr.Finkell said to try it."

"Damn! It's going to blow!"

"Watch out, Cody!"

Booom ...Fire! Fire!

"What the hell?!"

"Help me get him out of here. This place is about to blow! Evacuate! Evacuate! System failure! Evacuate all corridors at once! Evacuate! Evacuate at once!"

Boom!!!

"Call an ambulance! We need help over here! Oh, no it's Cody. Help! Help! Someone help me please."

"What is it, Sam?!"

"Cody's bleeding. He needs help! Over here!"

"Step back can you hear me, son?" "He's not responding! Let's get him to the hospital right away. Clear the way! Look out! Aaaaaaah!!! The smoke. Keep moving!"

"Wait! Where are you taking him?!" asked Sam.

"To Hawthorne Memorial Hospital. Hurry. Move it! Move it!"

The ambulance leaves in a hurry. (Woooowoooooowoooooo)

****

"Girl, look down there in front of the bank. Somebody got a serious limo. Daaamn."

"Ms. Ebony, I am here to drive you to the airport."

"What?!"

"Orders of Mr. Donavan."

"Where is he? In the limo?"

"No he is waiting in Atlanta for your arrival."

"I, I, I need to talk to Mr. Donavan."

"Hold, please."

"Yes. You have a limo here for me."

"Yes, how else can I get you to the airport?"

"You want me to leave now?!"

"Yes!"

"Well, what about my, my."

Ashley said, "I will take care of everything girl. Go, go, go. Girl, are you crazy? Go. I'll cover this for you!"

"But, but." "But, my ass. Go get out of here!"

"What about Cody?"

"If he calls, I will take care of it. Now go!"

"Right this way, pretty lady."

"I got to call Cody. Shit, shit my phone is dead."

"Your ticket is in the console of the limo pretty lady."

"Ooooo, hello, Mr. Donavan, I didn't know I was leaving today! Now! Right now!"

"Time is money, and money is time, as they say. We will take good care of you and bring you back in one piece. I promise you."

Ring. Ring.

"I am trying to locate Ebony?"

"Who is this?"

"This is G.E. Fiber Chips."

"I'm sorry, she is not in. Please call back later during business hours. Bye, bye."

"But!"

Click!

"Ooooooo! That isn't nobody but Cody checking up on her. Go on, girl, and get that money. He will be here when you return. Shit," said Ashley.

"What happened?"

"They hung up. Here comes another ambulance. Over here! Over here quick hurry!"

"What happened?"

"The boiler blew up! I tried to pull as many out as I could."

"Can you hear me? Check his vitals. He's going into shock, everyone stand back! We can't wait! On three—1, 2, 3—lift! Let's go!"

"Where are you going?"

"To Hawthorne Memorial Hospital. Let's go!"

"Oh my God! Oh my God! What should I do? Mr. Boles did you need me to call someone or do something?" asked Sam.

"We will take care of it. Can you drive?" asked Mr. Boles.

"Yes! Go ahead to the hospital and let them check you out with the rest of the crew."

"Yes, sir!"

"Hey! Check on Cody."

"I will."

"Doctor Ridge! Paging Doctor Ridge! Code red!"

"Excuse me! Excuse me!" said Sam.

"Yes, may I help you?"

"I am here to check on someone who was sent in an accident from G.E.!" said Sam.

"We have a whole emergency room full of G.E. employees," said the nurse. "What's his name?"

"Cody Walls."

"Are you family?"

"No. Yes. I mean, is he in the emergency room?!"

"Check down the hall to the right," said the nurse.

"Thank you! Thank you, so much!" said Sam. "O my God! Cody, are you alright?!"

"He can't hear you. He has been sedated."

"Well, is he alright?"

"He has lost a lot of blood and took a bad blow to the head. We are waiting for his x-rays to come back. Are you the wife?"

"Aaaaah, no I work with him."

"We need a next of kin for information."

"Ahhhh you can call our job. I'll write the number down."

"Thank You."

"Can I stay with him?!"

"I am quite sure they will be moving him to a room as soon as the doctor writes the order, so, sure you can stay."

Ring. Ring.

"Hello! Sam, this is Mr. Boles. How is Cody?!"

"He is not good. They said he lost a lot of blood and hit his head."

"Stick with him, and I will try to call his family."

"Okay." "Yes, sir!"

"That dumb-ass Finkell, this is all his fault. Oh, Cody, hang in there."

****

"Hey! I need to cash my check. Where is the cute, little black girl that cashes my checks?"

"She is out of the office today."

"Did you hear about the big explosion at the plant down the street?"

"No, what explosion?"

"The one that makes them computer chips just went up in flames."

"Oh, no! That's where Cody works. Was anyone hurt?!" asked Ashley.

"I'm not sure, but, it was a mess—ambulances were everywhere. Smoke, fire, cars, and people running all over the place. That is surely going to make the news. Just terrible. Just terrible."

"I got to go!"

"What about my check?"

"Next teller will help you!"

Ring. Ring.

"Ashley, this is Ebony. I can't reach Cody on his phone. Has he been in the bank today?"

"Aaaah, no girl, you know Cody, he is probably tied up. Aaaah, what's up with you girl?! Are you a star, yet?"

"Ash, this is the bomb. I have my own room. I mean sweet. Limo to and from the photo shoots, and maid service day and night."

"Oooooo. You go girl!"

"Can you give my number to the hotel to Cody when he comes in to cash his check?"

"No problem, boo."

"Ashley thank you so much. I could not have done this without you pushing me. Thank you so much."

"Just make me your manager when you blow up."

"Okay, ha, ha,ha,ha."

"Oh, I got to go. I will give Cody the message. See yah!"

Click!

"What have I done?"

Ring. Ring.

"Hello? Is this Ashley, Ebony's friend?"

"Yes."

"This is Mr. Donavan. I need a little favor from you, and I will make it worth your while."

"What do you need?"

"Well, I need you to keep Ebony's boyfriend out of the way for a few days, so I can close this photo shoot for Ebony. Can you help me?"

"Well, I don't know."

"I tell you what. Give me your bank account number and I will send you a little incentive for your effort and hard work."

"Well, okay, it's 11102379."

"One moment, please. Take a look at your account now and see if this will suffice. If there is problem, feel free to call me back. Deal."

"Wow, ahhhh, deal, deal. You the man, Mr. Donavan. Ha, ha, ha."

"Yes. I am. Well, ta-ta for now."

"Oh God, what have I done?! If I lie, I will hurt Ebony and Cody, and if I don't lie for Mr. Donovan, I don't know what in the hell he will do to my black ass. Okay, get yourself together child, right now. I got work to do."

Ring. Ring.

"Hello?"

"Ashley, have you heard from Ebony, yet? asked Ms. Valentine.

"Aaaah, yes ma'am, she just hung up. She sounded terrible—cold or flu—one of those things you know. Umm, I thought you were in a meeting, or I would have forwarded the call to you. Maybe we should send her some flowers or a card. Oooo, I will take care of it right away. Don't you worry, Ms. Valentine, just leave it to me. Wow I don't know if I can keep this shit up."

"Did you see this in the paper? There was a big explosion at the computer chip business on 110th Street. Isn't that where Ebony's boyfriend works?"

"Yes, I was reading something about that."

"I wonder if Ebony knows about it."

"I,I,I, told her about it when I talked to her this morning, and she said she will call and check on him right away."

"Maybe I should go over and see how he is doing."

"No! I mean, no, you have a meeting; I mean a conference call at one o'clock. Did you forget?!"

"Oh, you know, you are right. I left the notes in my car. If I hurry, I can run down and make it back in time."

"Yes, yes, do that. I will stall them if they call."

"Ashley you are an angel."

"Hurry, hurry."

"Okay, thanks."

"Whoooo, that was a close one. Let's see. Call the hospital and check on Cody!"

Ring. Ring.

"Hawthorne Memorial Hospital, may I help you?"

"Yes, yes, aaah, this is his girlfriend—I just heard about the fire. How is Cody?!"

"Well, here is the doctor now."

"Hello."

"Doctor, how is Cody? My God, I am a nervous wreck."

"Well, he is in pretty bad shape. He has a concussion, cracked ribs, and burns on his body, and he has lost a lot of blood just to name a few things."

"Damn! I mean this is terrible. I will get there as soon as I can."

"That's fine."

"Oh, thank you, Doctor, so much."

Click!

"One down; one to go."

Ring. Ring.

"Mr. Donavan?"

"Yes."

"This is Ashley. How long will Ebony be there?"

"Why?"

"Is there a problem?"

"Aaaah."

"Didn't I pay you to handle the problems on that end?"

"Yes, Mr. Donavan. I will handle it."

"Don't call again! I will contact you! Do we understand each other?!"

"Yes, sir! I am sorry, sir, this won't happen again, sir."

"Good!"

Click!

Oooooooh. Beep. Beep.

"Hello!"

"Wow! What is your problem?"

"Ebony!"

"Yes."

"Oh, I am glad to hear from you. I was about to call you girl."

"How is it going?"

"Okay, but, I am calling because I have not heard from Cody. Is everything alright?"

"Yes, yes, I just talked to him, and he said to tell you that he is very busy because of an explosion."

"Explosion?! Was he hurt?"

"No, no, did I say explosion? I meant exposition to the chips or something like that, girl. He is alright. He told me to tell you that he will be very busy trying to get things back up and running and he will give you a call."

"Why didn't he tell me that?"

"Oh, you know Cody when he gets into his work, girlfriend."

"Well, if he calls back, tell him to call me."

"I will try to call him and give him the message."

"Well just give me the number and I will call him myself."

"Oh, girl, it is so busy out there you will be on hold for hours. I will take care of every thing. He will be calling you by tonight I promise."

"Thanks, Ashley. You are the best friend a girl could have."

"I got your back. Handle your business. Bye, bye."

Click!

"Woooo, shit. This is about to drive me crazy trying to keep all these phone calls separated. I need a drink. This is too much. I am stepping out for a few. Hold my calls. I will be back soon. Chow."

"Hi, Ashley where have you been girl?"

"I have been trying to get in touch with you about that fine ass man at the club last week. Ha. Damn, girl, you look like you saw a murder or something."

"What?!"

"Just kidding, girl. What's been up with you, Ashley?" "Girl you don't want to know. Give me the strongest drink you got!"

"Damn it's one of those days, huh?"

"You don't know the half."

"Well, can I help?"

"Not on this one."

"Don't tell me he is married."

"No, no it's nothing like that. I wish it was that easy, shit."

"Ooooo, look over there at that fine ass mother fucker. Ashley, Ashley. Earth, earth to Ashley—are you there?!"

"Girl, I got to go!"

"What about your drink?!"

"Drink it."

"Okay, thanks."

"I don't know how much longer I can take all this lying and shit. I got T.D. on my ass, Ebony out having the time of her life at my expense, Cody about to die—not to mention lying my ass off to my boss—and covering up for everybody except myself, and wait a damn minute, who in the hell is this Sam woman that keeps calling me? She is asking a lot of questions. Maybe I should just say the hell with all this shit and let it blow up in everyone's face. No, they all would kill me. Damn, damn, damn."

CHAPTER 3

"Cody can you hear me?!" "Cody can you hear me?!"

"Doctor, why isn't he responding?!"

"He is in a coma."

"Is he going to be alright?"

"We won't know anything until his test returns."

"Oh, I have got to call my job and tell them what is going on."

"There is a phone on the wall through that door."

"Thanks."

"Hello, Mr. Boles?"

"Yes."

"This is Samantha calling from the hospital for Cody."

"How is the poor boy?"

"He's in bad shape, sir."

"Look, stay with him, it is a mad house here. Keep me informed. Anything you need, charge it to us."

"Yes, sir, I will do what I can. Let me get back before something happens."

Beep. Beep. Beep.

"What's happening?"

"We have got to operate at once! We are losing him!"

"Miss, you will have to leave the room."

"What?! What's happening!"

"Please get out now!"

"Cody, Cody, Cody, wake up, wake up!"

"Someone get her out of here now!"

****

"Mr. Donavan?"

"Yes, Ebony."

"I thought I was finished with the shoot."

"So did I, but, I just got off the phone with one of the top European magazines who wants to fly you over, all expenses paid, for a glamour shoot for their magazine. Isn't that great?!"

"What about my friends, and family?"

"Ebony, if you do this shoot, you can take care of your whole family for life."

"I must make a call first and I will be right back. Cody, where are you? Maybe he took some one to the hospital from the accident."

Click.

"Hawthorne Memorial Hospital. How can I help you?"

"I need to speak with. . ."

"Hold, please."

"What the. . . That does it Mr. Cody Taylor. You don't miss me! Well, I will show you! Mr. Donavan, book that trip! Let's go, let's get the hell up out of here now!"

"That's my girl, I will take care of every thing. Yes, yes, yes, everything ha, ha, ha. Everything is working perfectly. I will be rich and little Miss Ebony will be my cash cow. Ha, ha, ha, ha. Oh thanks, Ashley. Whatever you are doing is working. Ha, ha, ha, ha. I will deal with you later, my pretty."

"Can somebody tell me where is Ebony? I have been trying to get in touch with her all week!"

"Sorry Ms. Valentine, but, I have been holding her messages on my desk because you have been so tied up. She is out with a bad, bad virus, and the doctor told her it will probably take a week or so to clear up."

"That poor child, we must do something for her. Oh, thank you, Ashley, what would I do without you?"

"Shit! Shit! Shit! This is getting too confusing. Keeping everyone straight and separated. Ebony from Cody; Cody from Ebony; is Cody waking up; Ms. Valentine from seeing the magazine until Ebony can make it big, and speaking of Mr. Big—keeping that TG,TB, or TD whatever his name is happy. It's just too much! I am going crazy as hell! I need some damn help myself."

****

Beep. Beep.

"Hello?"

"Ebony, this is T.D."

"Yes."

"I have great news!"

"What is it?" "Not only are you going to London, but I have booked you for Paris and Spain photo shots."

"Yeah, thanks."

"Aren't you excited?!"

"Yes, but I have to make a call."

"Sure, sure, you probably want to tell all your family and friends.

"That's it. . . . bye." Click.

"Ashley, girl where are you? I need you now!"

Beep. Beep.

"The party you are trying to reach is not in. Shit! I will try the bank. She has got to be there please!"

"World Bank, Ashley speaking, how may I help you?"

"Ashley! Ashley!"

"Yes."

"O, thank God! I have been trying to reach you for days. Where have you been?!"

"Where have I been?! Where have I been?! I have been like a switchboard trying to keep everyone's lives from crossing and it has been pure hell!"

"I know, I know, I know, but, I have been so busy that I have not had a chance to even look at a telephone, much less talk on one. I don't know where to start."

"Well let me start for you. I thought you were just going out for a day or two, and it turned into a month! I have been lying to this one and that one to cover for you, and now you call saying that you don't have any time? Girl, please!"

"Ok, ok, where is Cody?!"

"He, he, he's working lots of overtime because the plant had an explosion."

"Explosion?!"

"When?! Where?! How?! Is Cody all right?!"

"What have you been doing? I told you all of this. What the hell have you been doing or drinking over there. When will you be back? Hold on, I have someone on another line."

"Wait! Wait! Don't put me on hold!"

Click!

" Oooooo. Damn it, damn it, damn it!"

"World Bank, Ashley speaking, how may I help you?"

"Yes, this is Mr. T.D. I am calling for another favor, my dear."

"Oh, hello, Mr. T., what can I do for you, sir?"

"Ebony will be trying to contact you. It is very important that you make everything sound peachy, or it could cause problems, and we don't want problems, now do we?"

"No, sir! I will take care of everything, sir."

"I know I could count on you, and as a token of my appreciation, check your bank account. I'm sure you will be pleased."

"Dammmmn! Thank you, Mr. T.D. Sir, and trust me, I will take care of all, aah everything."

"Good, ta-ta."

CLICK!

"Stupid child, don't she realize with her account number I can take the money back anytime I want? Ha, ha, ha."

"Oh shit, Ebony are you still there?!"

"Yes, was that Cody?"

"Ahhhh no, Ahhh yeah, yeah, that was him! He said don't be mad with him. He will explain it all to you tonight when he calls you."

"How is he going to call me when I am not calling on my phone?"

"Girl, have you got lost in the times? I have caller ID. I will call him and give him the number, and he probably will be so excited that he will call you before nightfall. Ha,ha,ha."

"Okay."

"Bye!"

"Wait! Don't put me on hold again!"

Sorry please hang up and try your call again.

****

"I keep getting paid like this, I can quit the banking business and become a counselor. Ha, ha, ha. I have got to get in touch with Cody right now! What is that number to the hospital? Here it is."

Dial.

"Hawthorne Memorial Hospital. This is Gladys speaking, how may I help you?"

"Yes, could I speak to Cody Taylor?"

"One moment please."

Ring. Ring.

"Hello?! Is that you, Cody?"

"No this is Sam."

"Sam. Who is Sam? Sam who?!"

"Oh, I work with Cody. Is this his girlfriend, Ebony?"

"No."

"I work with Cody, and they have me staying here with him since the accident."

"Well can I speak to Cody?"

"Cody has been in a coma for over three weeks."

"Damn. Well, I work with Ebony and she has been out of town, and she asked me to call and check up on him. Has there been any change?"

"None, none at all."

"Good."

"What?!"

"No, I mean good you are there with him. Ebony has been so worried! Look, ah Sam, right?"

"Yes."

"Write this number down and call me if there is any change in Cody's stay in the hospital."

"Okay. But, shouldn't I be telling this to Ebony?"

"No, she is hard to get in contact with sometimes, so it is much easier to contact me instead."

"Your name is what again?"

"I am Ashley, a very close friend of both Ebony and Cody, so you contact me only, okay?"

"Sure, Ashley thanks for the help."

"Oh don't mention it, girl. We girls have got to stick together."

"Right!"

"Bye, bye."

Click.

"Sucker, this is easier than I thought. Ha, ha, ha, ha, ha," laughed Ashely. "Now I thank I have finally got everything in place. Damn, I am good. Ebony will thank me when this is all over. This calls for a night on the town to ease my mind. Since I have all this money, I might as well enjoy the perks. I deserve it as hard as I have been working. Thanks to all you, I am rich."

CHAPTER 4

"Ashley, I want you to meet Tasha Bond. She is the replacement for Ebony. I am tired of waiting for her to come back to work."

"Ms. Ashley, will you call housekeeping and have them come and clean out my new office? Thank you. Let's do lunch while I wait, shall we?"

"Who does this bitch think she is talking to?! Ashley call and get my office cleaned. Next it will be clean my suit or make my coffee."

****

Doctor Thurman to O.R.! Doctor Thurman to O.R.! Code blue in room 129. Code Blue in room 129.

"Cody, please wake up. Please! There is so much to tell you. Wake up! Wake up, damnit!"

"Ooooooo, my head."

"Cody!"

"My head. What happened?"

"Cody, you are awake! You are awake! Yes! This is a miracle!"

"Where am I?"

"Wait! I have got to get the doctor! Nurse! Nurse! He is awake! Hurry! Please hurry."

"Let's see. Can you hear me?"

"Yes."

"What do you remember?"

"Nurse, someone called me. I am Doctor Hyatt."

"Doctor, he just came out of a coma."

"Let me examine him. I see this is good. Let's get him in for a CT scan ASAP!"

"Oh, I must call, ahhh, what is her name. Ah, here it is—Ashley."

"Hello, is this Ashley?"

"Yes, who is this?"

"It's me, Sam."

"I don't know any Sam!"

"Remember from the hospital, you said to call you when Cody wakes up?"

"Oh, yeah, how is he doing?"

"He is awake!"

"What?!"

"He is awake! It just happened a few minutes ago! Isn't it great!"

"Wait! Wait! Have you told anyone else about this?"

"No."

"Well, good!"

"What?"

"No, I mean while he is awake. I will call Ebony at once and tell her the good news."

Click!

"Damn! What in the hell am I going to do now that this fool has woke up! Think! Think! Ah, call Ebony? No. Ah, call Mr. T.D.? Hell, naw! I need some time to figure out this shit but what! I got it! I have got to find out where in the world is Ebony and what is she up to! Girl answer this phone before I kill you. No she didn't send me to her voicemail. SOMEBODY HELP MEEEE!"

****

"Hi T.D.!"

"Ah, Ebony, you are back! How was your trip?"

"Ooo, okay, I guess."

"You have been to some of the most beautiful countries in the world and that is all you can say?!"

"What's been happening around here?" "Calls have been coming in for you every minute to book you for shows, movies, and books."

"None from anyone else I take it?"

"You mean your boyfriend? I'm afraid not."

"It doesn't matter. I am through with him anyhow. Poof!"

"Well, I think I have something to cheer you up. There is a party at one of my friend's home tonight and everyone that's everyone will be there. Will you go with me, please? I promise you will have the time of your life!"

"Why not, I don't have anything else to do."

"Good! I will take care of all the arrangements. You will be the hit of the party! I will send the limo for you tonight."

"Yeah, yeah, yeah, I hear ya."

****

"Sam, this is Mr. Boles. Where is Cody?"

"They have taken him for some tests, Mr. Boles."

"You said that he was awake?!"

"Yes isn't it great!"

"Yes, I thought the poor boy was a goner for sure from the looks of that fire."

"Mr. Boles, is there anybody that I can call and let them know about Cody's condition?"

"Well, there is his girlfriend at the bank, but I am sure she already knows by now."

"Oh, yes, some girl that works with her has been keeping her informed of his condition. Where are his parents?"

"They were killed in an automobile accident some years ago."

"That's terrible. I am going to talk to the nurses to see if it is anything I can do. I'm going to the bank and meet Ashley. Maybe she can tell me where to find his friend."

"That's a good idea. You go, and I'll stay and keep an eye on things here go, go."

****

"Well, Ms. Valentine this is a very nice restaurant."

"Tasha, I only eat at the best of the best, girl. Ha, ha, ha. What the?!"

"What is it!"

"That girl looks like Ebony!"

"Ebony who?"

"My Ebony from the bank!"

"You mean the woman I replaced?"

"Hell, yeah! No way, she's at her family home because of some problem or another. It can't be. I must be loosing it. This is one of the top magazines—no way it could be her. Wow, what an amazing resemblance; my God they could pass for twins."

"She's alright, but I've seen better."

"Yeah, I guess you're right. Besides, she is too homely to pull off such a move. Ha, ha, ha, ha."

"True that."

****

Ring. Ring.

"Ms. Ebony, your limo is outside to take you to the evening's festivities."

"Thank you. Tell them I will be right down."

"Ahhh, don't you look fabulous."

"Thank you, T.D. You look divine yourself."

"Tonight, you will eat the best, drink the best, and be the highlight of the evening, my dear!"

"Oh, my God, look at this beautiful mansion. It's like a giant dream!"

"Come my dear, let's party!"

"Good evening, may I take your wrap?"

"Please. Thank you."

"Refreshment?"

"Yes, please. Look that's Bill Cosby! Ha, ha."

"Why yes it is."

"Is that Oprah?! Dammn! Hello. You are Doug Wonder, quarterback of the Chargers!"

"Yes, may I have this dance?"

"GO! GO! Enjoy yourself, Ebony."

"Ha, ha, you got some bad moves, Mr. Quarterback."

"You got some bad moves yourself Miss…"

"Ebony."

"Ah what a beautiful name for a beautiful woman."

"Can I cut in?"

"DJ Ding!!! You are one of the most popular rappers in the game."

"WOW! Not only are you pretty, but smart too! Ha, ha, ha. What, are you a dancer?"

"No, I model and plan on getting into acting soon."

"Cool, I feel you, I feel you. Let's get a glass of champagne, and I will introduce you to my manager."

" Would you really do that?!"

"No problem, just let me get the drinks," then DJ Ding mumbles, "I will fix this bitch." As he returns to the table with drinks, he says to Ebony, "Here is a little something-something to get you right, boo. Cheers to the new star!" DJ Ding mumbles, "She won't know what hit her." "Shall we? Right this way."

"Oooo, my head, that must have been a strong drink."

"Ah you just starting to party. Let me help you mama!"

"Wait! What are you doing?!"

"Cool out, I won't hurt you. Here, take this, it will make you feel better. I take them for headaches all the time."

"Thank you. The room is spinning. Ooooo. I, I, I,…."

"Come lay down. You probably had a little too much to drink."

"Maybe you're right. Wait! Wait! What are you doing! Stop! Stop it! No! No! NO!"

"Mmmmm."

"Stop! Nooooo!"

"Shut up, bitch! You know you want it!"

"Help! Help! I, I, I, ..."

"Ahhhhhh."

"Damn it! Get off of me!"

"Shut up!"

"I,I,I,I"

"Ahhhhh, oooo. Yeah." Kiss! "Thanks, whatever your name is. I got to get the hell out of here before someone comes! Bitch sleep tight. I gots to go. Ha, ha, ha, ha."

"Oooooooo, help! Help! Someone help me please!"

"Shut up!" Smack! Bop!

"Ouch, my hand."

"That will shut you up bitch! I'm outte five thousand! See ya—wouldn't want to be ya."

****

"Oh, my God! Someone call an ambulance! Quick! Oh shit! Hang in there! Who could have done something as evil as this to this poor girl. Call security at once!"

"Oooooo, what happen to her?"

"Get out! Everyone just get out now! This is terrible! Ah, man, damn."

****

"Welcome to World Bank, can I help you?"

"Yes, I am looking for Ashley."

"Ashley Wyatt?"

"Yes, I think that's her name."

"Fourth door on the right, room three, ma'am." Knock. Knock.

"Ashley?"

"Yes."

"I am Sam."

"Oh, yeah! Come in, come in. How is Cody?"

"Better, but, he is a long way from being alright. I am trying to get in touch with Ebony."

"I forgot to tell you she has not gotten back from her trip."

"Where did she go? I really need to talk to her."

"She should be back late this evening. Give me your number and I will have her call you."

"Thanks, here it is."

"I will give it to her the minute she walks through the door."

"Okay, bye, bye."

"Forget that wench! What do I look like her secretary! She must be dreaming. Oh Ebony, where are you girl… where in the hell are you!!!!! I have got to call Mr. T.D. because I need some answers now!"

Dial.

"You have reached the office of T.D. Promotion. Leave your message after the beep."

Click!

"Damn! Where is everybody? This is getting too heavy for me."

"Morning, Ashley."

"Morning, Ms. Valentine."

"Ashley, can you collect all of Ebony's things and send them to her house because she is history."

"Yes, right away Ms. Valentine. I am going crazy—Cody knocked out, Ebony is missing, T.D. won't talk to me, this girl Sam is asking questions that I can't answer—I can't take this shit! I am not putting up with this bullshit. Let them all get out of this on their own and leave me the hell alone."

****

"What's going on?"

"Some woman upstairs just got raped!"

"What?! Who?!"

"T.D., its Ebony!"

"What? Oh, my God! When, where, who!"

"Make way! Make way! Emergency crew!"

"Ebony what the? I am so sorry, Ebony. I'm so sorry! I never should have let you out of my sight! My God! I will find out who did this and have them killed! Call the police! Call the police got damn it."

"Police! Nobody leaves until told to do so!"

"Officer, I' am with the girl in the ambulance. Can I go with her to the hospital, please?! Please! Sir!"

"Okay. Tommy go with them, and don't let them out of your sight."

"Yes, sir!"

****

"Cody!"

"Hey where am I?"

"Man, I don't know where to start. Ah, do you know who I am?"

"Yes, you're Sam from the job."

"Good, good. Cody, you were in an explosion at the work site, and you've been unconscious for over two months."

"What!?"

"Yes."

"Does Ebony know about it?"

"I can't seem to find her anywhere! I have called your friends and they can't seem to locate her at work or at home."

"Well did someone call the police?"

"No, but I did get in touch with your friend, Ashley at the bank, and she stated she was out of town on business and will give her the message when she returns."

"Wow! I have got to get out of here and help Ebony!"

"You can't leave. You are not well."

"I can't just sit here and do nothing."

"Okay, okay, I will go to the bank and talk to Ashley and see if she has found out anything yet, but, Cody, you've got to promise me that you will stay right here until I get back. Alright?"

"Alright, go! Just go! I'll be all fine."

Ring. Ring.

"World Bank, Ashley speaking, how may I help you?"

"Ashley, this is T.D."

"Well, finally, Mr. T.D. I have been trying to get in touch with you for days!"

"Shut up! Just shut up and listen. Ebony has been hurt."

"What?! What happened?!"

"Don't worry about it. I will take care of it."

"What do you mean you will take care of it? What happened to Ebony?!"

"A small accident, but, I am taking care of it. Listen, if any one comes around asking questions about Ebony, tell them she is fine, but she has to stay in California for a few more days."

"Now wait just a minute. I am sick and tired of covering for you, and I am not going to do this anymore. You hear me?!"

"Bitch, have you forgotten about all that money I put in your account?!"

"Damn the money! Where is my friend?!"

"I told you that she is fine, and I will take care of everything."

"That's not good enough. I am going to call the police if you don't tell me what is going on!"

"I don't think you want to do that because I have friends everywhere, if you know what I mean, and if you go to the cops you are in this too, baby girl, so do what I say and stay cool 'till you hear from me. Bye."

Click!

"Ooooooooo!" "If you need to make a call hang up and dial again..."

****

"Hi, Ashley. It's me, Sam. Have you heard from Ebony yet?"

"Why is everybody asking me about Ebony? I am sick and tired of hearing about Ebony, Ebony, Ebony. You all are making me sick about Ebony. Just leave me the hell alone about some damn Ebony!"

"I was just checking for Cody because he has been asking about her."

"This is a bank—not a damn lost and found office. Okay? Now get the hell out of here! Now! Before I call security on your ass! Do you hear me?! Get the hell out of here! Move it—now! Do you hear me?! Get out! Shit on this Shit it's driving me crazy as hell! Niggers threatening my black ass. I didn't ask for none of this shit. Fuck it all got damnit! Slam! And stay out!"

****

"Ebony, can you hear me? It's T.D. Can you hear me?"

"Ooooooo. Where am I?"

"Ebony, sweetheart, you ran into a little problem at the party."

"What kind of problem?"

"You, you, were raped."

"What?! What?! Did you say raped!"

"Baby, baby, baby, just listen; calm down. I will take care of it, don't you worry. Don't worry! Don't worry!"

"Nigger, where were you when I was getting raped? Ha! Now you talking about you are going to take care of it?!"

"Ebony, if this gets out, you will be just an average model.

"Average model? Average model? What am I? A school project? Ha! If I keep my mouth shut, you will give me an A! Is that the way it works T.D.? Ha! Is that it, mother fucker?!"

"You don't understand."

"I don't understand?! Well, I tell you what I do understand is that I was with you at some fucked up party and I was rapped! Is that understanding enough for you, T.D., or maybe you are going to be like some gangster and go out and shoot up the town. Is that it? Tell me!"

"Now just a minute, you were working in a bank making petty cash. I made you a star!"

"Star my black ass. Forget that I am going to sue every damn one of you. Star! Star, my ass! At what cost T.D. did you think of that motherfucker! Ha!"

"I will fix it, Ebony. I promise you!"

"Fuck this shit. I am out of here right now!"

"Ebony, Ebony, wait, wait, damn, shit!!!!!! I have got to fix this before it gets out of hand. Hello! Give me Lisa Savage now!"

"One moment please."

"Hello, Lisa!"

"Yes, who is this?"

"This is T.D. I need you to fly down to the A.T.L. -- RIGHT AWAY! I will tell you all about it when you get here."

"Okay, T.D., I m on my way. Just stay cool. I will take the next flight out. Sounds like something big is happening in the A.T.L. He sounded desperate. Book me the next flight to Atlanta. Hurry!"

CHAPTER 5

"Cody, I don't know what her problem is, but, your friend, Ashley, almost took my head off when I asked about your friend Ebony."

"Don't worry about it. I am through with Ebony. Let her keep on doing her thing, and I am going to do mine."

"What are you saying?"

"Mmmmmmm. My ribs."

"Cody, are you sure about this?"

"Sam, you have been there from the beginning to the end and that is the kind of woman I want with me."

"But, I don't know what to say."

"Don't say anything; let's just go home."

"The doctors have not released you, yet."

"I feel like a cripple."

"You are lucky to be alive."

"Well how are we doing, young man?" asked the doctor.

"Doc, can I go home now?"

"Wow, not so fast. You have sustained some serious injuries from that fire. To be safe, let's see how you look in a few days."

"The doctor knows best, Cody."

"Yeah, alright. You win. Aaaa."

"See."

"Cool."

****

"T.D., I got here as fast as I could. You sounded like you had big problems."

"Lisa, I don't know how to handle this one. Sit down, and I will tell you the whole story from start to finish!"

Ring. Ring.

"Hello?! Hello?! Who is this?!"

"This is Big Mo from Bush Wack Records. I am calling to see if I can use your girl in one of our hip hop videos?"

"What?! What?!

Who?"

"You know—your girl, Ebony."

"Aaaa, I will have to get back with you on that. I am swamped right now."

"Okay, player, but don't wait too long."

"Right, right; I got ya."

"Who was that?" asked Lisa.

"Ah, ah, nobody, he will call back."

"T.D., I need you to take me to the house where this alleged rape took place."

"Aaaa, okay, sure let's go. Wait! Let me tell my office how to get in contact with me in case I get any calls from Ebony."

"Where is she?"

"Aaaa—out. Let's go."

****

"Home at last!" exclaimed Cody.

"Take it easy cowboy. You are not out of the woods, yet. Remember what the doctor said—take it easy."

"I will, and thanks again. I couldn't have done it without you, Sam."

"No problem, you would have done it for me."

Kiss.

"I feel better already. Ha, ha, haa."

" Hey! Wow! Cody, you have a nice place here."

"I have put a little work into getting it just right— you know what I mean?"

"Yes, very nice."

"Let me show you around. This is my den."

"Nice."

"This is my kitchen."

"Oooo."

"This is my living room." *Slamming door.* "I call this my sound room—where I come and just listen to music."

"Mmmm, nice, very nice."

"And, this is my bedroom, where I, I, I, Mmmmm."

"Wait! Are you sure you want to do this, Cody?"

"Yes, yes, a thousand times. Yes! Haaaa. Mmmmmm……………"

Kiss. Kiss.

"Cody, I hope you will not regret what we did later."

"I only regret that I did not do it sooner than later, Sam."

Ring. Ring.

"Hello, Cody, this is Mr. Boles. I have a new super hard drive that just came in, and I will need you and Sam to come in as early as you can tomorrow to set it up. Are you up for it?!"

"Yes, sir!"

"Oh, can you get in touch with Samantha and let her know?"

"I think I know where I can get in touch with her. I will take care of it. You can rest assured, sir."

CLICK!

"Well, duty calls. Looks like we have a big job starting tomorrow at work. Are you ready partner for the big job?"

"Sure boss, anything you say. Ha, ha, ha, ha."

"Come with me let see if you can earn your next raise. Mmmmmmmmm."

"Ooooo, Cody, you bad, bad boy."

THREE WEEKS LATER

"T.D.! Where are you?!"

"Hello! Hello! Anybody home?!"

Ring. Ring.

"I guess I have been reduced to secretary now," said Ebony.

"Hello! Yes, this is Big Mo from Bush Wack Records. I was calling to see if T.D. has talked to Ebony about making the video with one of our rappers."

"What?! What?! Aaaaa, hold please!" Ebony mumbles to herself, "T.D., you sorry mother fucker -- trying to put me out of work—ha! I will fix your ass; just watch me." As Ebony returns to the phone, she replies, "Oh, yes, she has been cleared for that shoot. Just send the fax to this e-mail address, and we will take care of the rest."

"Kool, look forward to seeing her as soon as possible. Later. Peace!"

"Now, let's see what you think of this Mr. T.D. I am taking my own jobs from now on. Ha,ha, ha. Ms. Ebony—promoter—ha! How you like me now!"

****

"Mr. T.D., I need to get with Ebony and hear her side of the story," said Lisa Savage.

"She is scheduled to fly in today, and the minute I see her, I will bring her directly to you."

"Okay, I have to call my office. They're getting me some info from the hospital and on this rapper from the party we have been following."

"Lisa, or should I call you Miss Savage. . . ha, ha, ha. . . I don't know how to thank you."

"Back up. Down big boy—one big dog for now is enough to catch."

"My bad. Oh, I see here on the answering machine the promoter from Bush Wack Records called. I am trying to get Ebony in a video shoot with one of his rappers."

Ring. Ring.

"Just a moment, T.D. I need to take this."

"By all means—go right ahead."

"Yes. Good. Fax it to me right away good work! Keep in touch, Sarah. Bye. T.D., I have got to go I'll be in touch later."

"Good bye."

Slam!

"I hope I did the right thing by calling the cops on this man. Something just doesn't feel right about this one."

Ding. Dong.

" Hello! Yes my name is Detective Lisa Savage. I am here to talk with a Mr. D.J. Ding."

"Just a moment. I will buzz you in."

"I, I, I, . . . I am Big Mo, D.J. Dings' manager. What is this all about?"

"I just need to ask him some questions about where he was the night of the party at the Johnson estate."

"What you want an autograph or something we can send that to you?"

"No. Is he here?"

"No, he went out shopping for outfits for the upcoming video shoot."

"Well, I will leave my card. Could you have him call me?"

"Okay, cool." "What the fuck is wrong with that bitch. She tripping big time. She must think she is Pam Grier or some damn body. She gone mess around and get capped asking questions. Oooo, I got to call that model and give her the starting date. Where is that number...here it is."

Ring.

"Hello?!"

"Yeah, is this Ebony?"

"Yes."

"Well, this is your lucky day. You have been picked for the upcoming D.J. Ding video shoot."

"Are you serious?!"

"That's on everything I love baby girl!"

"Ooooooo, when, where, what do I have to do!"

"Woah, woah, woah, slow down, sweetie cake. Let me talk to your manager, and I can set everything up."

"No, No, No, ah, I will be handling this one myself because I don't want this to get messed up—you feel me?!"

"Cool with me. I will send you all the info tonight, but I need your e-mail address."

"Great! I will be waiting. Bye, bye." "

Okay, peace, Boo!"

"Yeah, who needs T.D.—forget that sorry ass nigger. I will show him that I can take care of myself. I don't need him for nothing! I trusted him before and look what it got me. Well T.D., see ya! Ha, ha, ha, ha."

CHAPTER 6

"Hi, Cody."

"Oh, hello Ashley, how's it going?"

"Okay, I guess. You still seeing Sam?"

"Yes, we make each other very happy. Have you heard from your friend Ebony?"

"Not in a long time."

"That figures—she always was a selfish wench."

"That's not true!"

"What's not true about it? She left her boyfriend, her job, her friends, and never looked back! Forget that bitch I have a life."

"Cody, you don't understand."

"No, I understand—it's alright. She used me, but that's cool. Well, here comes my ride. Later, Ash."

"Oh shit, I have got to get in touch with Ebony before it's too late, or am I already too late."

Mmmm. Kiss.

"Hi, babe."

"Wasn't that Ashley you were talking to?"

"Yeah, she was just kicking it."

"I have some great news for you. I just came back from the doctor and I am pregnant."

"What?!"

"Are you mad?"

"Hell, no. This is great! How! When! I mean I know how. Ah, how far long are you?"

"Slow down, stud, I am just a couple of weeks and everything looks good."

"Wow, this is the greatest thing that ever happened to me! I promise you I am going to be the greatest dad in the world to my little girl."

"Or, boy!"

"You right. I love you and you love me and that's what starts a family. Haaah—ain't no stopping us now. We are going to be the new Waltons—in the hood—ha, ha, ha, ha."

"You go bad boy. I hear ya."

Kiss. Kiss.

Ring. Ring.

"Hello."

"Cody, this is Miss. Valentine from the bank."

"Yes, is there a problem?"

"Well, I was reviewing old files and saw that your and Ebony's account is still open and what would you like to do with it."

"Wow, ain't that a trip. I tell you what you can do Miss. Valentine. You can close and burn that account because I will be in to open a new account for me, my new wife, and my soon-to-be baby."

"What?! Congratulations! That is great. I look forward to hearing from you and your new family. Bye, bye."

"Everything alright baby?"

"Couldn't be better, baby."

****

"Hi, boss, I'm back from lunch."

"Oh, hey Ashley."

"Anything happening that I should know about?"

"Well, now that you ask, you remember that cute young man Cody that used to go with Ebony?"

"Yeah."

"Well he and his new wife are having a baby."

"What?! You can't be talking about the same Cody that went with Ebony!"

"Yes, I am."

"No you ain't!"

"What's with you? He probably just moved on. What's the problem?"

"What's the problem?! What's the problem?! Babies, wife, marriage. Where is all this coming from? I just saw him down the street, and he didn't say none of this to me."

"Ha! Probably because you can't keep anything with your big mouth, ha!"

Ashley mumbles, "I got to make a call to T.D. right now!"

"Who is T.D.?"

"Ah, nobody. Talk to you later."

Dial.

"Answer the phone jive ass nigger."

"Hello!"

"T.D.!"

"Who is this?"

"T.D., this is Ashley."

"Ashley who?"

"Ebony's friend from the bank."

"Oh yeah, what is it?"

"I need to talk to Ebony right away. This is urgent!"

"What is it?!"

"Man, I can't tell you. This is a woman thing!"

"You tell me or you can lose this number!"

"Wait!" "Okay." Ebony needs to call me because her boyfriend is about to make a terrible mistake if she doesn't talk to him as soon as possible!"

"That's it! That's your big problem. You are crazy to call me with some bull about a boyfriend. Do you know it cost a hundred dollars a minute just to talk to me, and you call with some soap opera shit like this?! Bye!"

Click.

"Ooooooo. That's it! I am through with all their sorry asses. Ebony, T.D., Cody, Sam, and all of these mother fuckers. If I never see any of them again, it will be too soon. Fuck it. First Commerce Bank, Ashley speaking, how may I help you today?"

"Ashley, this is Ebony."

"Who?!"

"Ebony."

"Okay, how can I help you today?"

"Ashley did you hear me? This is Ebony, damnit!"

"Ebony, Ebony, Ebony -- is that you? I mean is this you?!"

"Yes, it's me."

"Bitch, you got a nerve. I have been trying to get in contact with you for a long time, and you just blew me off like I ain't shit and now you want to talk. I should hang up on your country ass."

"Will you shut up and listen for a damn minute! I know that I have hurt a lot of people, and I am sorry, but, that's not why I am calling you. Girl, I am going to be in a big-time rappers video shoot."

"Ebony, are you crazy? You have bigger problems than a damn video."

"Ashley, I thought out of all my friends, you would be happy for me, but, you are just like all the others—jealous of me."

"Jealous! What have I got to be jealous about covering for your ass, or lying to everyone, so that you can go out and play star. Ha! You tell me, Ebony!"

"No, forget all of you."

Click.

"Oooo. She got a nerve to hang up on me and I'm running around like a damn fool. Okay, I am hitting the breaks on all this shit. See ya, and I wouldn't want to be yah! Don't come back to me crying the blues because it will be too late."

CHAPTER 7

"Ebony, I have been looking for you everywhere. Was that the call from a guy name Big Mo?" asked T.D.

"No, just a friend or used to be friend. What's up?"

"I have someone here to talk to you about the incident at the party last month."

"What? I don't need that right now."

"Ebony, I am Detective Lisa Savage. I have been working on your case, and I need to ask you some questions while they are fresh in your head."

"Didn't you hear me? I said not right now, not ever!"

"Ebony, come back!"

"Let her go! She is probably still in shock," said T.D.

"I will try again later when she is more relaxed. Well, I have a meeting with someone I will talk with you later. Bye."

"Good bye, Ms. Savage. I got money to make. Let me get bizzie!"

****

"Hello! T.D. Productions. Is this a soloist or a group? Well, send me a demo and I will let you know what I think. Okay, bye now. Sucker."

Ring. Ring.

"Big Mo."

"What's up, Mo, this is T.D. You didn't call me back on that video. What's up?!"

"T.D., we go back a long way other than that I would have took the bitch and ran with her."

"Who are you talking about? Ebony?"

"Yeah, your girl is making deals behind your back, and you need to put that in check, my nigger!"

"What?!"

"Yeah, she not only booked the shoot—I have a signed contract on my desk."

"What?!" A nasty little mother. Good look out, Mo.

"Wait! What about the shoot?"

"It's still on, and I will make sure of it."

Click.

"A nasty little bitch. Two can play that game. Ha, ha, ha, ha, ha."

****

Ding, dong.

"Who that?!"

"Detective Lisa Savage."

"Oh, you again? What's up?!"

"I need to speak with a Mr. D.J. Ding."

"He ain't here!"

"Listen, I am not one of your little groupies. I will haul every one of your asses downtown and keep you there for hours! You dig?!"

"Whoa, little lady, there he is coming up the driveway now."

"What up, dog? You got your broads talking to you on the steps now, show some class—invite the little lady in."

"Yo! Ding, she is here to see you."

"Look, boo, you need to wait in line like the rest."

"Don't you mean like Ebony?"

"What?! Who in the fuck is Ebony?"

"My name is Detective Lisa Savage, and I am here to ask you some questions about a party you were at in Beverly Hills about a month ago."

"I don't remember no party. You need to talk to my lawyer."

"Fine, I will call for a police car to pick you up and we can finish this down town."

"Whoa, whoa, whoa, we don't need all that. What kind of questions you talking 'bout?!"

"Where you at Cool Steve's party on June 10, 2009?"

"Oh, hold up—you for real with this shit, ain't you?! I didn't bring nothing to that party, and that's on everything I love! What in the hell is going on here!"

"D.J.! What are you doing?!"

"Shut up! Do you know who this is? Ha! She said she wanted to ask me about some party! I ain't done nothing at no party!"

"Detective, we will set up a date and time for any of your questions, but he cannot answer any questions without his lawyer present."

"Fine, I will be waiting. Here is my card. I will be seeing you very soon. You gentlemen have a nice day."

"Are you fucking crazy?! What the hell did you say to that bitch, huh?" asked Big Mo.

"Man, she was talking about locking me up and some mo shit!"

"Locking you up for what?!"

"Some Ebony or Emily—I don't remember what she said the name was."

"Nigger! You don't talk to no police—that is my job! Shit. What else?"

"That it, then you came in."

"Okay, okay, I got this. I got this."

"Who the fuck is Ebony?"

"Man, some bitch that was at Cool Steve's party."

"What she selling, buying, or what?"

"No, no, somebody raped the bitch."

"What?!"

"And, now, they think it's me! Fuck that shit! I ain't going to jail for no bitch!"

"Cool it, my nigger, cool it. I have a plan to take care of all this shit in one whop."

"I ain't helping kill no bitch, Big Mo."

"Look nigger, just leave it to me."

"How you goanna find this Ebony whatever?"

"Nigger, I been working on this shit long before you knew anything about it. Not only am I going to get the bitch, but I already have the fall guy to take the hit for getting rid of the ho."

"Who that damn dumb?"

"Her manager, and the good part is he won't even know what happened. Ha! Ha! Ha!"

"Aaaaah, you a smart mother fucker, man. Now what—we gone kidnap the bitch?"

"No, no, she is going to come to me."

"Nigger, have you been hitting the woola?! How she just gone walk right in here no questions asked?"

"Check this shit—she has a signed contract to do the shoot for the video."

"What?! Why are you going to use that bitch? She is hotter than fake money!"

"Nigger, that's our alibi. Shit. When she gets here, we do everything just as we planned. Shoot the video and after it is over, we smoke the bitch and place the gun in T.D.'s car. Ha, ha, ha."

"That's some smooth shit Mo, for real." "I'll drink to that!"

****

"Dumb asses. You have got to step up your game on technology. I just planted three bugs in your house while you two were arguing. Dumb asses, and I got every word that you said. Lisa Savage always gets her man, or should I say thug. Ha, ha., ha. Now let me get back to Mr. T.D. and see what part he is playing in this little thug game."

Beep.

"Yes, Lisa Savage speaking."

"Lisa! T.D. here. How are things going on your end?"

"It's moving slow, but it's moving."

"Good, I want to hear every detail."

"Chat with you later. Peace."

"Oh, you will definitely be hearing from me—you can count on that, my brother. I need to find this Ebony before Mo and his thugs kill this poor girl. Where is that contact number? Yes got it!"

Ring. Ring.

"Hello."

"Ebony?"

"Yes, my name is Uma, and I am with a top movie company, and we would like to talk with you about being in a movie."

"Did you say movie?!"

"Yes."

"Hell yeah! I mean, I might be interested."

"Great! Can you meet me at the Blue Parrot in about an hour?"

"Sure, I think I can make it."

"Wait! No managers. We want to just talk and get a feel of how you read before the final decision is made."

"I agree. He is out right now. Anyhow, I can handle it." Ebony thinks to herself, "I told you T.D. I can handle my own bookings. You are just in the way."

"Okay, see you soon."

"Fine, see you soon—ta-ta."

Click!

"This girl is a walking victim for these thugs. If I don't save her, she will be dead before she knew what happened. I have got to move fast. I will go back to the hotel and set up everything with the team. We will see who has the last laugh, Mr. Mo."

CHAPTER 8

Knock, Knock, Knock!

"Ashley!"

"Ebony! Wa! Wa! What are you doing here?"

"Girl, I have been through hell, but, that can wait. I came all this way to talk to you about some very important things!"

"That will have to wait. I have a meeting to get to."

"Can't that wait?"

"Hell, no! Look, wait for me here until I get back, and I will hear all about it."

"What?! Are you crazy! If T.D. finds out that I am here, he will kill me!"

"If I don't get to this meeting I will kill your ass for him. Wait! What does T.D. want to kill you for?"

"That got to do with some of the shit I have to talk to you about damnit!"

"Girl, look, go up stairs, down the hall, and that's my bedroom. Stay there until I get back. No one is here, so you have nothing to worry about."

"How long are you talking about?"

"Not long. Just take a nap, and I will wake you up when I get back."

"Wait!"

"Bye, bye. I don't want to be late!"

Zoooooommmm.

"I don't like this shit, but I could use a quick nap, shit, I am tired as hell so cool."

As Ashley wanders throughout the house, she exclaims, "Damn! This girl has got it going on; this crib is fine as shit. Oh this bed feels good as hell. Ah, she had better wake me up as soon as she gets back here, so we can fix this crazy shit going on. Oh, no, Moet! Give me a shot of this shit. Um, um, um, that is some good shit. I am gonna drink all of this, hell, I deserve it after all the shit they have put me through. Yeah, I'm going to stretch out for just a few minutes and get myself together."

T.D. returns. "Ahh, home at last. Let me check and see if Ebony made it back yet. Ebony, Ebony! Ashley! What in the hell are you doing here?"

"Waa Waa, what, who dat?"

"What in the hell are you doing here? And where in the hell is Ebony?!"

"Oh, it's you."

"Damn right, it's me!"

"Where is Ebony, and how did you get in here?"

"Whoa, boss man, first of all, I am tired of all ya'll yelling and screaming at my black ass. I don't want anymore to do with this shit. Fuck the money, the drama, and all this shit."

"You do what I tell you to do! I gave you good money for your troubles."

"T.D., you can take the money and ram it up your ass because I did not ask for any of this shit!"

"Well, that is too bad because you can't get out."

"What you mean? I don't work for you or any of ya'll mother fuckers!"

"Where is Ebony?"

"I don't know."

"Where is she, bitch?!"

"First of all, I ain't nobody's bitch, and if I did know, do you think I would tell your sorry ass? You have ruined that girl's life."

"Get out of my house!"

"Get your hands off of me!" Smack!

"Bitch, are you crazy smacking me in my face! I will break your damn neck!"

"Turn me loose! Turn me loose! Get your hands off me! Help! Help!"

"You know what? Fuck this shit!"

Bang, Bang!

"Now what you going to tell bitch?! Oh, man I got to clean this shit up now."

Dial.

"Yeah."

"Yo! This is T.D., I got a little something I need you to get rid of."

"When?"

"Now—tonight!"

"Yeah, tonight! I'll pay."

"You know the price."

"No problem get here quick!"

"Take it easy; take it easy. We on the way!" Click!

****

"Hello! Ebony! I have been trying to get in contact with you all day. Where are you?"

"I have to meet a friend, and I will be back as soon as I can."

"Bye."

Click!

"That bitch, she thinks she is smarter than me. Ha, ha, ha. We will see about that. Ha, ha, ha. Yeah."

"Hello! Welcome to the Blue Parrot. May I seat you?"

"Yes, I am meeting someone."

"The name?"

"Uma."

"Ah, yes, right this way."

"Uma?"

"Yes, and you must be Ebony. Please sit."

"Wait a minute, I have seen you somewhere, aren't you that detective lady?"

"Yes, but, Ebony, I needed to talk with you about your case."

"You called me down here for some bullshit case that I told you I was finished with that mess."

"Ebony, we believe this guy that did this to you has done this several times before, but, we need your statement to stop him, or he will strike again."

"I told you I don't remember anything!"

"We showed his picture to the staff, and we have statements from the maid that saw you both go into the room that night, and a waiter that heard screams from the room and saw him leave in a hurry out the back way right after you were spotted with the door open lying across the bed and they called for help."

"I am out of here!"

"Wait! Wait! Ebony, you could help save a life and get this scum bag off the streets."

"I ain't no cop and I don't need this drama in my life."

"Okay."

"Hello. What! When? Thanks. Ebony this is not a game. Your friend Ashley was just found in an alley tonight shot several times," said Lisa.

"What?! You are lying! You are lying! I just left her!"

"Where?"

"She was at my house, and I told her I had a meeting and that I would be right back. That was the last time we talked."

"Was anyone else at the house?"

"No, everyone was gone."

"Just as I thought."

"What?!"

"Your friend T.D. is in this some way and I need to find out how."

"Wait. I believe you. What do you need me to do?"

"Ebony, right now, it is very important that you stay cool as if you don't know anything, and I will handle the rest. Trust me."

"Okay, now tell me everything—you know from the beginning up 'till now, with this becoming a model to being at that party."

"Sure. Wait! If they did this to Ashley, how will you protect me?"

"We have you watched around the clock, so you will have nothing to worry about, plus, I have placed bugs throughout the house at all locations with video."

"I have a video shoot next week. Should I go to that?"

"I know all about that and we have done the same at that house. Listen, Ebony, we can help each other, but these are very dangerous men, and we need you to trust us. We can nail these fools. It is very important that you just act normal. I will handle everything."

"Wow, this shit is freaking me out!"

"Ebony, we have been working this case for a long time, and this is the closest we have ever gotten to solving this ring of thugs, and with your help, we can put them away for a long, long time."

"Okay, this is what happened."

"Wait! I must record everything for court purposes."

"I understand."

"Okay, go ahead with your statement. ....Ebony, this is the tenth young lady that this same scam has been ran on, and after you become famous, they take your money, fame, and sometimes your life. Others become their slave for life because they sign the contracts without reading or understanding them. The bad part about it all is if you don't go along with their game, something bad happens."

"How bad?"

"Put it this way. What happened to your friend is just like a normal day's work for them."

"Why haven't they been caught?"

"Ebony, they are very good at what they do. This is it. We have enough to arrest them all, but, it all depends on what you do at this video shoot."

"I understand."

"Can you do it?"

"These sorry mother fuckers killed my best friend, and that's why I want to do it. Damn right—I can do it!"

"Good girl, we will be right there with you all the way. I promise you."

"Let's get these sorry asses."

"You go, girl!"

CHAPTER 9

"Yo! Yo! Yo! What's up Big Mo?"

"What it is, Ding? We straight for that shoot tomorrow or not!"

"My nigger, after this shoot tomorrow, we are going to be swimming in cheddar like all the big dogs, baby!"

"Hold up dog. You mean this bitch just gonna walk in here and get played and won't know a damn thing about it?!"

"Please my nig—have I ever let you down?"

"No." Well I got this dog. What about that cop bitch asking all them questions?"

"Man, T.D. got that bitch running around in circles like a fool. By the time she even thinks she knows what's up, we will be counting the stacks of cold hard cash, and she will be eating doughnuts in some doughnut shop with the rest of them punk ass cops. Ha, ha, ha."

"Yeah! Yeah! Yeah! That's right!"

"Look, I got to jet. I got a little honey coming over tonight, you know what I mean, dog?"

"I feel you. I feel you."

"Well, peace, I'm out of here."

Ring.

"Hello, Goon, this Big Mo. Meet me at the club tonight, so we can get this thing I been telling you about straight."

"Hold up. We still talking the same price that we agreed on?"

"You know that I have never reneged on no deal you ever done for me man! Where this shit coming from?!"

"Cool it, mother fucker, cool it. I just had a deal go bad with a nigger cross town, but I will fix that."

"Fuck that shit! I ain't no low life nigger cross town, this is Big Mo!"

"Haaaa right, right, right, cool Mo."

"I need to take a little break with some fat sweet boos. You feel me?"

"Yeah, look I will be there."

"You still my nigger even if you don't get no bigger." CLICK! "Damn, does anybody trust anybody any mo these days got damnit! Shit!"

"Whoa! Look at the honeys up in here!"

"Damn!"

"Easy my nig, we got business in this mother fucker."

"Yes, there's my man. Look you float till I need you."

"Cool."

"The Goon. What's up baby boy!"

"Big Mo, sit down, take a load off. Drink?"

"Yeah, yo, give me a Manhattan."

"What you want, 'G'"?"

"Let me have a yack on the rocks. Make that a double."

"Yes, sir."

"At once."

"How's it going, dog?"

"You know big things popping, little things dropping you know." "Cool , cool, look, dog I got this bad little red bone coming for a video shoot tomorrow, and after the shoot, I need you to do your thing. You feel me?"

"What's the deal, man. Why not just pay the bitch and let her go."

"Well, you know, D.J. Ding!"

"Yeah, that nigger is the hottest rapper out there."

"Well, he raped the bitch and now we got to put her to sleep, or Ding could go down for a long bid, man, you feel me?"

"Whoa, hold up. Did she go to the cops for this shit?!"

"No! No! No! Man, you know I would never set you up on a dirty lick—brother, come on, now."

"Look you remember T.D."

"Yeah."

"He told the broad he hired a detective to check the shit out and she believed it."

"How are you so sure she believed it?!"

"Listen, man she is on her way here for the shoot tomorrow. That's how I know she fell for it like a ton of bricks."

"Well, I don't know about this one."

"Ah, come on dog, any crack head could have done this job, but I wanted it done right, you feel me?!"

"Alright, I will take care of it, but it will cost you double cuz. I ain't know all this before. If we see anything that don't look right, we gone—point blank—you feel that nigger!"

"Cool, it's gonna go smooth as ice."

****

"Did we get that, Teddy?!"

"Every last word, Lisa."

"Did you want us to pick them up right now?"

"No, let's get all the worms in the same can, and then we will squash them all at the same time. That waiter outfit worked perfectly. We planted the bug and those master minds never expected a thing. Dumb asses. Good work, crew, but, we still have work to do. Let's go. Booker, you stay just in case anyone else shows up for the big throw down."

"Got you, Lisa. I am on it!"

"Well let's put these punks where they belong—in the garbage!"

Beep.

"Hello, Ebony where are you?"

"I'm on my way back to the house. Is everything alright?!"

"Everything is going just like we planned it. All we need you to do is to act yourself and you will be just fine. Oh, and by the way put that cigarette out—it is bad for your health."

"What?! You can see me?"

"Surveillance has come a long way baby."

"WOW! No shit. I mean. I understand. Handle your business, baby."

"Got to go. See you soon"

"Bye."

"This is like some spy shit and I am in the middle of it all, and that ain't good. I got to call Cody and see if he can help."

Beep.

"Hello."

"Cody!"

"Yeah, this is Ebony."

"Why are you calling me?"

"I just wanted to tell you…"

"You can't tell me anything. It's too late, and don't call here again!" Click!

"A mother fucker. Well kiss my black ass, and your bitch, too! Fuck him, a sorry ass country mother fucker. He won't shit anyway."

"Ah, Ebony, where have you been?" asked T.D. "I have been calling all over for you. Are you all right?"

"Yeah! Yeah! I am alright."

"Okay, oh, your friend Ashley had to leave. She had to go back because she had some problems at her job that couldn't wait. I told her I would give you the message."

"That sounds just like Ashley—run in and run out—a bitch!"

"You also had a message from Big Mo. Something about a video shoot tomorrow."

"Yeah, I was going to get with you on that, but I have been so busy."

"No problem. Mo and I go back a long way, and he has filled me in on everything. I got to give it to you. You cut a hell of a deal with Mo. You must really know your shit, boo. The figures looked good money-wise. You go, baby. My girl has all grown up and doing her own wheeling and dealing. Ah!"

"It was nothing like that, T.D. I just took the deal because you were out with that lady dick!"

"I hope it was worth it while I am here doing your work for you."

"Wait!"

"Just a minute, bitch, you could never do the kind of shit that I do around this joint and don't you forget it. You hear me?!"

"Oh, no. I know that you just didn't call me a bitch! Nigger I will kill your country ass and you will never be seen again. You don't know me mother fucker!"

"Cool it, cool it. My bad, boo. Look, we both had a long day. I am sorry. Let's just get some sleep and go get that money in the morning. You forgive me? Please, please, with sugar on top."

"Right! I'm going to bed. Night."

"Night gorgeous. Sleep well. Bitch, you gone sleep."

****

"Well, well, well, if this isn't beauty and the beast. Ha, ha, ha. What's up T.D.?"

"Long time, no see. I see you still keeping a good taste in women. Ha, ha, ha."

"Yeah, yeah, you know me. Nothing but the finest, my nigger. Is everything on schedule?"

"You know dat man. You talking to Big Dough Mo. Stack it from the ceiling to the got damnit floor."

"Welcome. Everyone let's make movies and dough. Ha! Ebony, T.D., let's take our places. Please come, come, sweetheart, I need you to go with Steffi to make up."

"Right this way, Ebony. Very pretty."

"Yes."

"Talk to me dog."

"Everything is in place. Just as soon as she finishes the video, her ass is a memory."

"Good, good I want to wrap this up as soon as possible, if you know what I mean."

"Oh, shit, oh shit, I know that is not my soul brother number one, T.D., the big touchdown king of the rap word! Ha,ha,ha."

"Damn man, why you ain't tell me you were coming? I could have had some nice hotties waiting on you my nigger!"

"Ding, how has it been going my brother? I hear you got the hottest shit out there right now!"

"Well, you know what can I say. Ha, ha, ha."

"Yeah! Yeah!"

"Okay, places everybody. Let's do this! Music ready!"

"Ready!"

"Bring out the model on my queue. Alright. Lights, music, camera, action!"

"What's up ladies? What's it gone be? This the nigger that all the rappers want to be. Got big bank, big cars, living large. Just snap my fingers and I get all the broads. Okay, send out the model!"

"Ooooooo, damn, she looks good as shit!"

"Wait! Wait! Hold it. Just one damn minute. That's the son of a bitch that raped me!"

"What?! I don't know this bitch! Who the fuck she think she talking to! I will blow her mother fucking head off!"

"All units move in! All units move in now!"

Boom! Bang!

"Everybody on the floor now! Move it! Get down! Get down! On your face. Move and your next rap will be in hell mother fucker! Ebony are you alright?"

"Yes, yes, Lisa, thank you, so much! I didn't know that he was the guy that was going to be in the video! That sorry son of a bitch. I hope he rots in hell. I was scared to death!"

"You did just fine baby; you did just fine. Ebony you're bleeding."

"What?!"

"Oh my God! Get an ambulance now! Halt! Halt! Stop him! Stop him! Police!"

Screech. Zoooom.

"What happened?"

"D.J. Ding got away."

"How?"

"When we went to place the cuffs on him, he head-butted me and ran."

"This is just great! We had the killer and lost him. Well, what are you standing around for get out there and find him now! Go! Go! Shit! Did someone call for an ambulance? Yes over here! Ebony, listen, honey. You just concentrate on getting well, and we will get Mr. Ding I promise you." Kiss.

"You ain't got nothing on me cop!"

"Well, well, well, Big Mo. I have enough evidence to put you in prison until the walls fall down, and that is what I intend to do. Get this bum out of here."

"Lisa, Lisa, tell them I am not in this mess. I called you to clean up this mess!"

"You know what, T.D.? You are a disgrace. I can't stand to look at you, particularly when I think of all the beautiful young girls you just destroyed in your path. Prison isn't good enough for you. I should put a bullet right between your eyes. Ha! Ha!"

"Lisa, no! Lisa!"

"Don't worry, I wouldn't give him the pleasure of one of my bullets. Book him! I have got to get out of here. All these rats are starting to stink up the place!"

In the news. . . "Super model Ebony Chase was shot in a police raid in California today. She was taken to a nearby hospital and is in critical condition. Police stated she was the only one at the home for a video shoot. Also involved in the incident the famous rapper D.J. Ding who is at large for possibly participating in the incident and leaving the scene. Details at eleven."

"That is Ebony! What in the hell is she doing with a bunch of thugs. O my, God, she's been shot! She was trying to tell me something when she called and I blew her off. Wow, this is all my fault! I got her shot! I have got to go see about her. I have got to go now!"

"Cody, where are you? It's your lovely pregnant wife, you handsome man. Look at this. Cody, you are a sloppy man leaving your closet door open. Why is your suit case missing? Where are your clothes? Cody! Cody! Stop playing around! You are scaring me. Cody, come out here right now! Something is definitely wrong. I know he wouldn't have left without telling or saying something to me. He must have left a letter. Home town girl shot. Ebony Chase, Hollywood super model was involved in police sting in famous rap artist D.J. Ding's studio. The artist escaped from the scene and is currently on the run from police. Cody, no you didn't leave your family to run off for some airhead! What were you thinking? Are you thinking? Noooooo, Cody! You can't do this to me. Why? Why? Whyyyyyy?!"

****

"All of ya'll thought you had D.J. Ding, didn't you? But, I showed you mother fuckers that you can't stop me! I'm the baller, shot caller of the game. I'm going to get out of the country and start my game all over again. Wait! Before I go anywhere I am going to get even with this bitch that set me up! Ebony, your ass is mine!" D.J. Ding dials the phone.

"Hello. Yo! This is Ding."

"Nigger, you all over the T.V., newspaper, and everything. What in the hell you calling here for?!"

"Shut the hell up and listen! I gave you everything you got and now you trying to base on me. I ought bust a cap in yourrrr."

"Hold it. You still my dog. What's up?"

"I was set up, man. I ain't had nothing to do with none of that shit, you feel me?"

"Ya, ya, I got you."

"The only one that can pin this on me is the chick Ebony."

"Man she fine as…."

"Fuck that! We got to do her before she goes to court!"

"What?! Man, I ain't killing nobody man!"

"You don't have to do nothing, but watch my back. We go in and out before anyone knows what hit'em."

"When do you plan on doing this dog?"

"Tonight."

"Tonight!"

"Yeah, make the hit and fly out tonight that simple."

"What I get out the deal?"

"I will give you ten thousand dollars."

"Ten thousand dollars just to be a lookout!"

"I'm in dog."

"Okay, I will call you tonight and let you know when we move."

Beep.

"Hello, Lisa, it's Mat. It went down just like you said. Ding contacted some thug named RaRa, and he has agreed to help him finish the job on Ebony."

"Good job, Mat, let's not botch this one up this time. I want undercover all through that hospital now!"

"Got it boss. OUT!"

****

"Ah, nurse can I have something for the pain?"

"I will contact your doctor."

"What the? Cody! What are you doing here?"

"I heard you were shot, and you were trying to contact me. I felt it was all my fault!"

"Cody, no, this had anything to do with you, well yes it did, I mean no it didn't. Listen, this was a nightmare from the beginning."

"Are you alright?"

"No! I've been shot! Where were you?"

"Where were you?! I was blown up in a building, stuck in a coma, and almost burned to a crisp, while you were just wondering all over the place getting shot by thugs."

"Are you for real?! I tried to call you before any of this ever happened."

"What you mean you tried to call me. My number is still the same and has been the same since high school!"

"Well having it and answering it are two different things. I called, no answer, I left message after message, and no return calls."

"What messages, Ebony? And, what calls? I live in the same house, same e- mail, so don't give me that. You couldn't get me shit because that is a lie!"

"Oh, so I'm a liar, Cody? My friend Ashley is dead, and I guess that's a lie, too, right?!"

"What?! Ashley dead? When? How? Is she in this also? First of all she tried to contact you over and over, but she said you were always working, or can't get to the phone, or will call me back. Ebony, Ashley and I talked one time prior to me coming here, and she never told me any of this modeling or whatever you were doing."

"That's a lie! Don't you sit here and talk about my friend like that. She knew what you meant to me, so why would she make this up."

"Ebony, I swear on my baby's life."

"What?! Baby?! When did? Who did you have a baby with? Ashley?!"

"Nooo. I don't know where to start. You see."

****

"Hello, Ebony, I am Doctor Nash. I performed your operation to remove your bullet. How are you feeling?"

"Like I have been run over by a truck."

"This is to be expected for the next few days, but you should have a very good recovery."

"Thanks, doctor."

"Any questions?"

"When can I leave?"

"In about two days. We just like to play it safe and rule out infections."

"Thanks again, Doc."

"Good day."

Cody mumbles, "Man, this is moving too fast for me. People shot, people dead, what in the hell? I'll, be right back I have to make a phone call."

"Wait, Cody, I have not finished talking with you!"

"I'll be back! I can't pick up a signal in here. I'll try outside. Sam is probably having a fit!"

Ring. Ring.

"Hello. Cody?"

"Hi, Sam."

"Where are you? Are you alright?"

"I'm with Ebony."

"Ebony?! What the hell are you doing with Ebony?"

"Sam, it's a long story."

"So long you couldn't tell me you were leaving. Ha!"

"Sam, listen."

"No, you listen. When you can find time for your family, you come on back home if that is where you won't to be."

CLICK!

"Sam! Sam! Wait! Alright, Ebony I want some answers, and I want them now."

"Ah, back so soon. Did you put your fire out?"

"Ebony, this is no time for playing. Who shot you and why?"

"Hold on. I have some questions of my own, like where were you, and who's baby are you taking care of because it damn sure ain't mine!"

"So, I came all this way to hear sarcasm and for you to talk about me! You left me!"

"No! You made me leave you and you can leave right now! I don't need you. Go! And don't come back! I don't need this shit from you or anyone else!"

"Ebony, look let's start over please. I will go first."

"No! I will go first. I was at work and this man came in who needed a money transaction made. While we were preparing the transaction, we began talking. His name was T.D., and he gave me a job offer. I didn't give it a second thought. Later that week, he called again, but this time, he said he had found a job offer for me, and he could fly me out and back before anyone would notice I was gone. Ashley started talking about how I was missing the chance of a lifetime and big money, and just went on and on."

"So, this was Ashley's doing!"

"Wait! I'm a grown woman and I don't need anyone to make decisions for me, okay! I am not going into anymore of what happened because I have figured it out. You want someone to take the blame for your mistakes!"

"My mistakes! How's this my mistake?"

"Well, Cody, let's see. Never could get in contact with you, you never returned any of my calls."

"I never got any calls from you, Ebony."

"LIAR! I called thousands of times. I even had Ashley to try to get in contact with you, and she said you didn't have the time, or you were, quote, working. Yeah, I see what you were working on. Oh, ooo, don't forget HAD A BABY! Left me to 'fend for my own self! Is that enough sir, or shall I go on!"

"You wait just a minute! Don't you bring my baby in to your bull! Now, it's my turn. I got promoted and where were you to celebrate? I was blown up, put in a coma, burned, and almost died! Now, is that enough for you! All the while you were with your hoods or thugs, or whatever you call them. Oh, before you bring out your crying towel answer those questions!"

"You selfish, nasty, sorry ass man. Go! Get out! Get out and don't come back!"

"Cool, Ebony. You have ruined my life, had your best friend killed, and got yourself shot! You know, you're right. You don't need my help; you are doing just fine all by yourself. Kiss. Kiss. Have a nice life! Don't bother getting the door; I got it!" *Slam!*

Ring. Ring.

"Lisa Savage."

"Lisa, we have a fix on D.J. Ding."

"Good work. Don't move in. We don't want to scare him off again. Put a tap on the phone, and don't let him out of your site. We have confirmed that he is waiting for all his thug partners to arrive before they make their move on the hospital. I am placing the undercover agents in the hospital and all around Ebony."

"We will stand by for your call. Outta here."

"I have got to call Ebony and advise her of what is going to take place."

Ring. Ring.

"Hello, Ebony?"

"Yes."

"This is Lisa Savage. How are you doing?"

"I'm alright Lisa."

"You sound sad. Is everything alright?"

"It's a long story. Don't worry about it."

"Ebony, I have good news. We have located DJ Ding, and we will arrest him soon."

"Thanks, Lisa for everything."

"Hang in there. It's going to be alright. Ebony?"

"Yes."

"I need you to remember this. God doesn't make mistakes. What He has for you is for you and no one or nothing can change that."

"Thanks, Lisa. I needed that."

"Talk to you soon. Bye, and keep your head up."

Click.

"Now Mr. Ding, it's my turn to dance with you, my friend. Bring it on I will be waiting. Ha, ha, ha, ha."

CHAPTER 10

"Yoooo, what's up nig!"

"Yeah, yeah, what's cracking, baby."

"Did you have any problem getting here?"

"No, your man was right on time picking us up."

"You bring the guns?"

"Got'em right here."

"Come on in. Chill out. Drinks over there, and it's plenty of food in the frig."

"Whoa, man, that's the bomb smoke right there."

"You ain't never lied. Pass that Henny, my nig."

"Now let's get down to business. This bitch, Ebony, has got to go, or it's my ass, point blank."

"How you want to do it dog?"

"We just gone go in and smoke her ass."

"What?! That's your plan?! What about guards? Yeah, and cops?"

"Check this, we are friends of Ebony, and we are bringing her flowers."

"Man, have you snapped, what we gone do? Choke her to death with some fucking flowers? Ha, ha, ha."

"No, the guns will be in the flowers. We just ease in and smoke the bitch, and leave out the fire escape."

"When we rolling?"

"Tonight!"

Cough! Cough!

"Cool. Turn that jam up; that's my jam dog. Ha, ha!"

****

Beep.

"Lisa."

"Yes."

"The move is tonight."

"We will be waiting. I have a search warrant for the house. After they leave you and your men, go through the house and collect the drugs and guns. I'm sure it will not be hard to find."

"Be careful, Lisa."

"You too! OUT! Well as they say, it's show time!"

****

Eeeeek.

As DJ Ding and the thugs pull in to the hospital, DJ Ding says, "Alright my nigs, let's do the thing."

Over the hospital intercom, "Doctor Howard, code blue; Doctor Howard, code blue."

"Yes, may I help you?" asked the nurse.

"Yeah! I mean what room is Ebony Chase in?"

"Room 504."

"Thank you. Let's use the elevator."

"Lisa, they are on their way up."

"Got you. Thanks! Okay, you in that closet. Lloyd, have your men cover the fire escapes. You two behind the curtain, lock and load."

Gun click. Click. Click.!

"See what I told you. Easy as cake. The fire escape is right by the door. Ha, ha, ha. Smoke, you stay outside and keep a look out. Let's go."

Eeeeek, as the door opens slowly.

"Ah, sleeping, huh, bitch? Let me pull that sheet off your face because I want to see your face when I pop that ass. Yeah, Yeah. Surprise bitch!"

"Freeze! Drop it! Don't move! Police! Don't move! Police! On the floor! On the floor now! Move it!"

"What the?!"

"Surprised to see you, too, Mr. Ding."

"You got nothing on me!"

"Right, right. Bob did you get the other one?"

"Ten-four, Lisa. Got him trying to use the fire escape."

"Good work. Get this trash out of here. It stinks."

"You heard the lady; let's go. Move it! Now!"

"Ebony, it's over honey."

"Did you get them?"

"Yes, we got all the bums. Thanks to you, he will never see the streets again."

"Good. Thank you for everything, Lisa."

"No thank you, you were a brave young woman. Now baby, just get well. I will be in touch."

Kiss.

"Thanks."

The End

****

But wait. We can't end on that note:

1. What happens to Ebony when she leaves the hospital?

2. What happens to Cody when he returns to his wife Sam?

3. Will Sam and Cody stay together after this hold ordeal?

4. Will Ebony return to her home to find out about the baby?

5. Who is Sam and what is in her past that Cody doesn't know?

NOW WHO, WHAT, WHEN, WHERE, AND HOW WILL IT END?!

Special Thanks Goes To

1. GOD ALL MIGHTY FOR WITH OUT HIM I AM NOTHING: A MEN

2. My wife and best friend Kathy Lisa Hawthorne who never stop believing in me no matter what came our way.

3. My two children: my son, Christopher Michael Hawthorne, and my daughter, Stephanie Christina Gail Hawthorne—my rocks.

4. My Mother, Sarah Lucille Hawthorne, who spiritually pushed me to keep going and finish the book.

5. My second Mother, Mrs. Katherine Florence Pilson, who showed me the meaning of never stop fighting no matter what.

6. My brother, Sergeant Robert Landers Hawthorne, who showed me it's never too late to get started on your dream.

7. All my Pastors: Rev. Booker, Rev. Dr. Robert Allen Diggs, Sr.; Rev. Dr. A. L. Gee; Dr. A. Lincoln James; Rev. Allen; Rev. Mitchell; Rev. Elmus Morgan; and Rev. Mason.

8. All my brothers and sisters who saw me through it all.

9. All the doctors at The Medical College of Virginia who put me back together.

10. All my friends and along the way of my journey.

ENJOY EVERY WORD AND REMEMBER THIS FACT

"God gave everyone this same gift
It is up to you how you use it"

The Power to Choose What You Do!

Chris M. Hawthorne

"TRUST IN THE LORD IN EVERY THING"
YOU DO